The Fox and the Crane

How should you treat others?

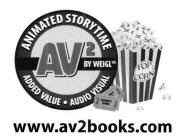

www.av2books.com

Go to **www.av2books.com**, and enter this book's unique code.

BOOK CODE

W228667

AV² by Weigl brings you media enhanced books that support active learning.

Published by AV² by Weigl
350 5th Avenue, 59th Floor New York, NY 10118

Copyright ©2013 AV² by Weigl
Copyright ©2010 by Kyowon Co., Ltd.

Library of Congress Cataloging-in-Publication Data

The fox and the crane.
   p. cm. -- (Aesop's fables by AV2)
 Summary: The classic Aesop fable is performed by a troupe of animal actors.
 ISBN 978-1-61913-109-5 (hard cover : alk. paper)
 [1. Fables. 2. Folklore.] I. Aesop.
 PZ8.2.F67 2012
 398.2--dc23
 [E]
                                2012018612

Printed in the United States in North Mankato, Minnesota
1 2 3 4 5 6 7 8 9 0 16 15 14 13 12

052012
WEP110612

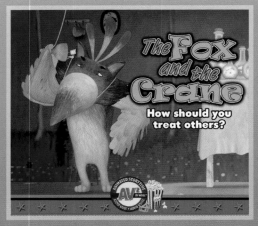

FABLE SYNOPSIS

For thousands of years, parents and teachers have used memorable stories called fables to teach simple moral lessons to children.

In the Aesop's Fables by AV² series, classic fables are given a lighthearted twist. These familiar tales are performed by a troupe of animal players whose endearing personalities bring the stories to life.

In *The Fox and the Crane*, Aesop and his troupe teach their audience to respect the needs of others. After they get a taste of their own medicine, the pigs learn to treat others the way they would like to be treated.

This AV² media enhanced book comes alive with...

Animated Video
Watch a custom animated movie.

Try This!
Complete activities and hands on experiments.

Key Words
Study vocabulary and hands-on experiments.

Quiz
Test your knowledge.

The Fox and the Crane

How should you treat others?

AV² Storytime Navigation

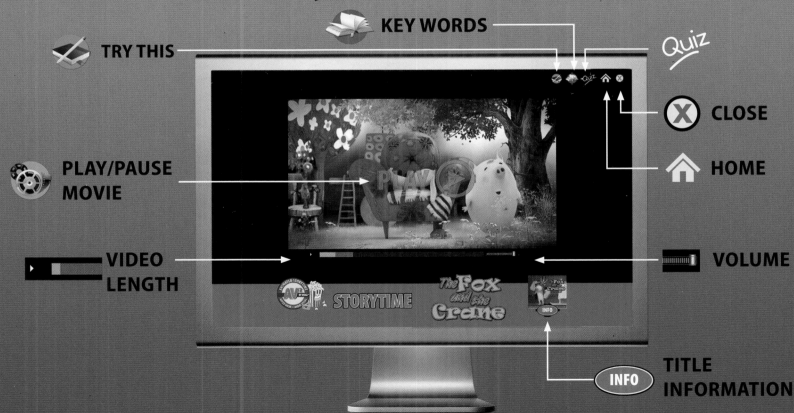

TRY THIS

KEY WORDS

Quiz

X CLOSE

PLAY/PAUSE MOVIE

HOME

VIDEO LENGTH

VOLUME

STORYTIME

The Fox and the Crane

INFO

INFO TITLE INFORMATION

3

The Players

Aesop
I am the leader of Aesop's Theater, a screenwriter, and an actor.
I can be hot-tempered, but I am also soft and warm-hearted.

Libbit
I am an actor and a prop man.
I think I should have been a lion, but I was born a rabbit.

Presy
I am the manager of Aesop's Theater.
I am also the narrator of the plays.

6

The Story

Aesop was worried.

"I promised to give everyone a present today!"

Aesop opened a big box in the corner of his carriage and looked inside.

"Let me see... I know it's somewhere!"

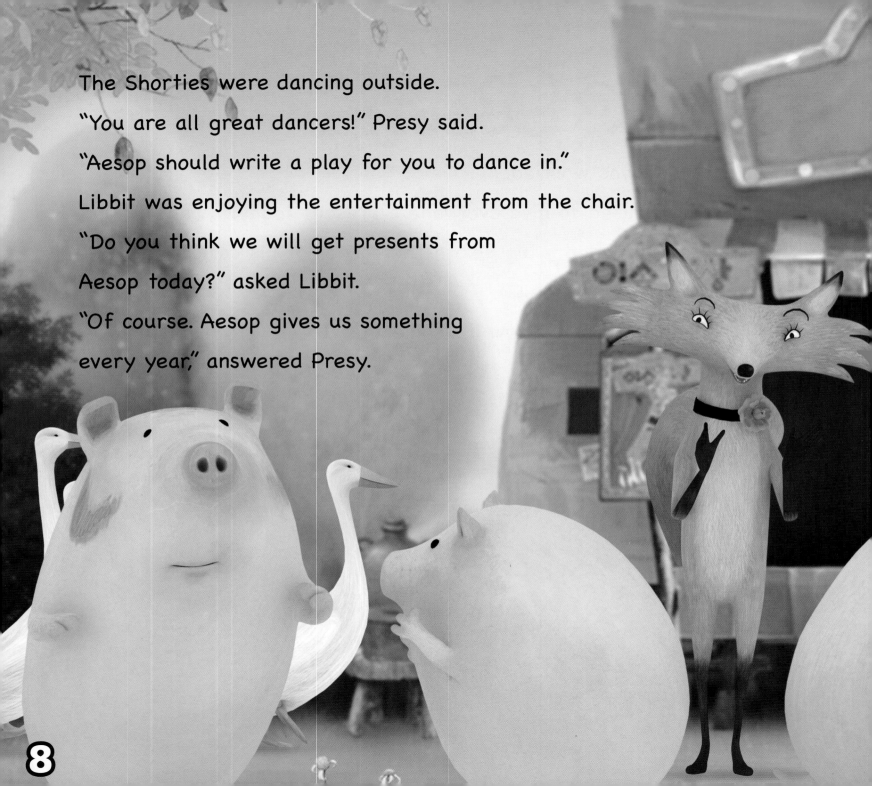

The Shorties were dancing outside.

"You are all great dancers!" Presy said.

"Aesop should write a play for you to dance in."

Libbit was enjoying the entertainment from the chair.

"Do you think we will get presents from
Aesop today?" asked Libbit.

"Of course. Aesop gives us something
every year," answered Presy.

9

When Aesop came out of the carriage, the Shorties and Libbit were excited.

"Umm," said Aesop. "These are the presents I got for you this year. I think you will like them."

Aesop gave the Shorties a box.

"To you, I give the latest farming tools."

The Shorties were given garden shovels and seeds.

Aesop gave Libbit a hammer and nails.

"Libbit, these are the latest building tools.

You can have fun making props with them."

Libbit and the Shorties were disappointed.

Presy said to Aesop, "It's not very kind of

you to give presents like these. We all

expected something we could play with."

This gave Aesop an idea for his next play.

That afternoon, Aesop announced his new play.

"The title is *The Fox and the Crane*.

I will play the crane, and the Shorties will play the pigs."

Libbit and the Shorties were still not happy,

but Aesop thought the play would cheer them up.

"Let's get started!" Presy said.

15

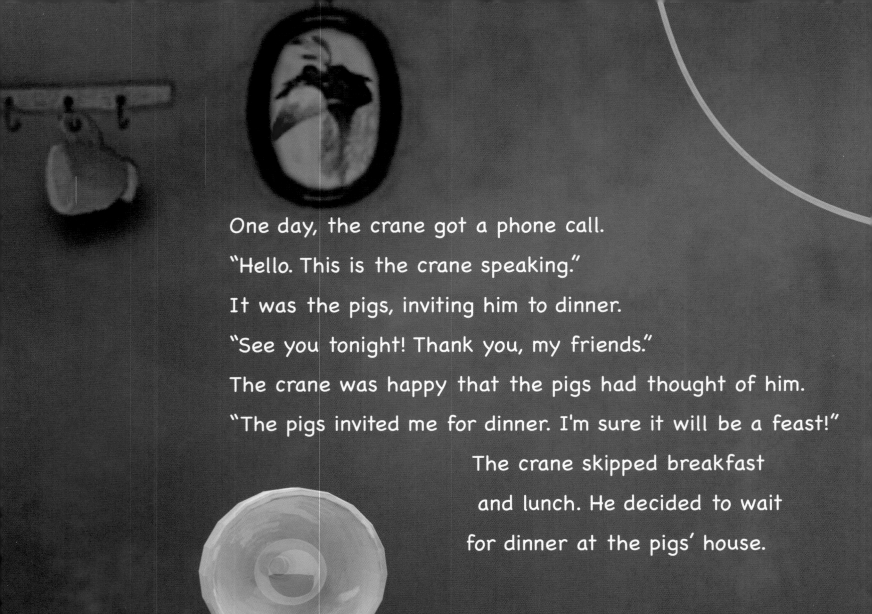

One day, the crane got a phone call.

"Hello. This is the crane speaking."

It was the pigs, inviting him to dinner.

"See you tonight! Thank you, my friends."

The crane was happy that the pigs had thought of him.

"The pigs invited me for dinner. I'm sure it will be a feast!"

The crane skipped breakfast and lunch. He decided to wait for dinner at the pigs' house.

When the crane arrived at the pigs' house,

he was invited to their table.

The pigs served soup and beans.

The pigs ate happily, but the crane could not eat

because the food was served in a flat dish.

One pig saw this, and asked the crane,

"Do you not like beans? Can I eat them?"

The little pig took the crane's food.

The pigs served spaghetti as a second dish.

The crane wondered how to eat it.

He tried winding it around his beak,

but he could not get it in his mouth.

He was angry, and his beak hurt.

A few days later, the crane invited the pigs over for dinner.

"I'd like to treat you all to a meal to thank you for your kindness."

The pigs rushed to the crane's house.

The crane gave each pig their dinner.

"Help yourself!"

The crane served the food in long-necked bottles,

but the pigs could not get the food to come out.

They tried turning the bottles upside down.

They even tried putting the bottles in their mouths.

Only the crane could enjoy it with his long beak.

"However hard you may try, you can't eat it.

You should have put yourself in my shoes."

The pigs went home very sad and hungry.

After the play was over, Aesop went to find the Shorties.

"I made dinner!"

Aesop found the Shorties lying on the floor.

The Shorties had tried to eat the food from the longnecked bottles, but were now tired from their efforts.

Aesop sighed, looking at The sleeping Snorfies.

"I thought you would try to eat it!"

Treat others the way you would like to be treated.

What is a Story?

Players

Who is the story about? The characters, or players, are the people, animals, or objects that perform the story. Characters have personality traits that contribute to the story. Readers understand how a character fits into the story by what the character says and does, what others say about the character, and how others treat the character.

Setting

Where and when do the events take place? The setting of a story helps readers visualize where and when the story is taking place. These details help to suggest the mood or atmosphere of the story. A setting is usually presented briefly, but it explains whether the story is taking place in the past, present, or future and in a large or small area.

Plot

What happens in the story? The plot is a story's plan of action. Most plots follow a pattern. They begin with an introduction and progress to the rising action of events. The events lead to a climax, which is the most exciting moment in the story. The resolution is the falling action of events. This section ties up loose ends so that readers are not left with unanswered questions. The story ends with a conclusion that brings the events to a close.

Point of View

Who is telling the story? The story is normally told from the point of view of the narrator, or storyteller. The narrator can be a main character or a less important character in the story. He or she can also be someone who is not in the story but is observing the action. This observer may be impartial or someone who knows the thoughts and feelings of the characters. A story can also be told from different points of view.

Dialogue

What type of conversation occurs in the story? Conversation, or dialogue, helps to show what is happening. It also gives information about the characters. The reader can discover what kinds of people they are by the words they say and how they say them. Writers use dialogue to make stories more interesting. In dialogue, writers imitate the way real people speak, so it is written differently than the rest of the story.

Theme

What is the story's underlying meaning? The theme of a story is the topic, idea, or position that the story presents. It is often a general statement about life. Sometimes, the theme is stated clearly. Other times, it is suggested through hints.

The Fox and the Crane

Quiz

1 What did Aesop give the Shorties as a present?

2 What did Aesop give Libbit as a present?

3 Why were Libbit and the Shorties disappointed?

4 What did the pigs serve for dinner?

5 What did the crane serve dinner in?

6 What did the pigs learn?

Key Words

Research has shown that as much as 65 percent of all written material published in English is made up of 300 words. These 300 words cannot be taught using pictures or learned by sounding them out. They must be recognized by sight. This book contains 118 common sight words to help young readers improve their reading fluency and comprehension. This book also teaches young readers several important content words, such as proper nouns. These words are paired with pictures to aid in learning and improve understanding.

Page	Sight Words First Appearance
4	a, also, am, an, and, be, been, but, can, have, I, of, plays, should, the, think, was
5	always, animals, at, do, food, from, get, good, if, like, never, other, them, to, very, want, with
7	big, give, his, in, it's, know, let, me, see
8	all, are, asked, every, for, great, play, said, something, us, we, were, will, write, you
10	came, got, out, these, this, when
13	can, could, idea, kind, next, not
14	new, started, still, that, thought, up, would
16	be, call, day, house, it, my, one
19	because, eat, he, saw, their, took
21	around, as, how, second
23	each, few, help, later, over, your
25	come, down, even, hard, home, long, may, only, put, they, try, went
26	after, find, found, had, made, now

Page	Content Words First Appearance
4	actor, leader, lion, manager, narrator, prop man, rabbit, screenwriter, theatre
5	dance, music, pig
7	box, carriage, corner, everyone, present
8	chair, dancers, outside, year
10	seeds, shovels, tools
13	hammer, nails
14	crane, fox
16	breakfast, dinner, feast, friends, lunch
19	beans, dish, soup, table
21	beak, mouth, spaghetti
23	meal
25	bottles, shoes
26	floor

Check out av2books.com for your animated storytime media enhanced book!

1 Go to av2books.com

2 Enter book code   W 2 2 8 6 6 7

3 Fuel your imagination online!

www.av2books.com

AV² Storytime Navigation

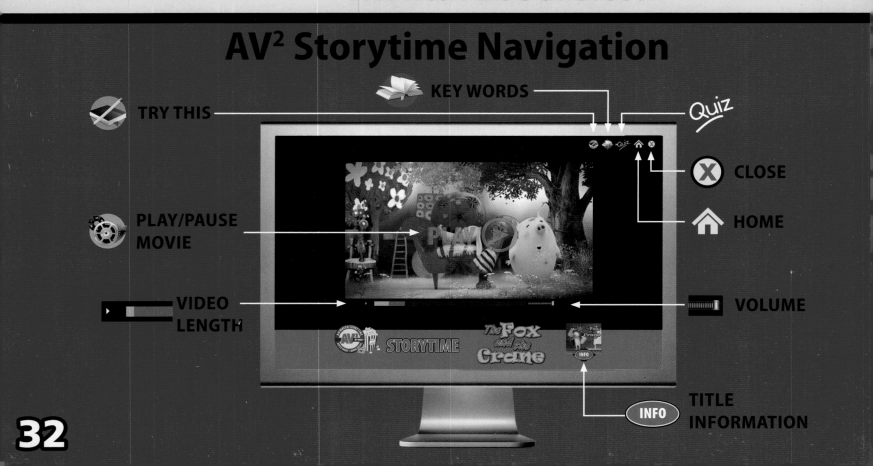

KEY WORDS

Quiz

TRY THIS

X CLOSE

PLAY/PAUSE MOVIE

🏠 HOME

VIDEO LENGTH

VOLUME

STORYTIME

INFO

TITLE INFORMATION